READING RAINBOW®
R E A D E R S

SPORTS STORIES

You'll Have a Ball With

SeaStar Books
NEW YORK

Special thanks to Amy Cohn, Leigh Ann Jones, Valerie Lewis, and Walter Mayes for the consultation services and invaluable support they provided for the creation of this book.

Reading Rainbow® is a production of GPN/Nebraska ETV and WNED-TV Buffalo and is produced by Lancit Media Entertainment, Ltd., a JuniorNet Company. *Reading Rainbow®* is a registered trademark of GPN/WNED-TV.

The following are gratefully acknowledged for granting permission to reprint the material in this book: Selected text and illustrations from "Jaws" from *Beezy at Bat* by Megan McDonald, illustrated by Nancy Poydar. Text copyright © 1998 by Megan McDonald. Illustrations copyright © 1998 by Nancy Poydar. Used by permission of Orchard Books, New York. All rights reserved. • Selected text and illustrations from *Kick, Pass, and Run.* Copyright © 1966 by Leonard H. Kessler. Used by permission of HarperCollins Publishers. • Selected text and illustrations from "Practice" from *Oliver and Albert, Friends Forever* by Jean Van Leeuwen, illustrated by Anne Schweninger. Text copyright © 2000 by Jean Van Leeuwen. Illustrations copyright © 2000 by Anne Schweninger. Used by permission of Phyllis Fogelman Books, a division of Penguin Putnam, Inc. • Selections from *Harry's Visit.* Text copyright © 1983 by Barbara Ann Porte. Illustrations copyright © 2000 by Yossi Abolafia. Used by permission of HarperCollins Publishers. • "Fast Track." Copyright © 1999 by Nikki Grimes. Used by permission of Curtis Brown, Ltd. • Selected text and illustrations from *Soccer Sam.* Text copyright © 1987 by Jean Marzollo. Illustrations copyright © 1987 by Blanche Sims. Used by permission of Random House Children's Books, a division of Random House, Inc. • "Night Game." Copyright © 1999 by Lee Bennett Hopkins. First published in *Sports! Sports! Sports!* edited by Lee Bennett Hopkins, published by HarperCollins Publishers. Used by permission of Curtis Brown, Ltd. • Illustrations on pages 53, 63, and 64 copyright © 2001 by Henry Cole.

 SeaStar Books • A division of North-South Books Inc.

ISBN 1-58717-085-X (reinforced trade binding) 10 9 8 7 6 5 4 3 2 1
ISBN 1-58717-086-8 (paperback edition) 10 9 8 7 6 5 4 3 2 1

Contents

Jaws

BY Megan McDonald

PICTURES BY Nancy Poydar

Play ball!

The Hurricanes were playing the Jets.

Beezy said, "We need one more player."

Sarafina rode past on her unicycle.

"Let's ask Sarafina Zippy,"
said Merlin.

Ben said, "She doesn't even have
a mitt."

"Meet Jaws," Sarafina said.

Her mitt had a shark face on it.

"Did you draw that?" Merlin asked.
Sarafina said,
"I can draw stingrays too."
"Batter up," said Beezy.

The Hurricanes were up first.
Beezy hit the ball.

Merlin hit the ball.

Lucy and Ben hit the ball.

Sarafina Zippy was up.
She closed her eyes.
Strike one!

"Keep your eyes on the ball,"
said Beezy.
The pitcher threw the ball.

Sarafina jumped out of the way.
Strike two!

Merlin said, "Keep your bat
in the air."
The next pitch hit Sarafina's bat.
It landed in the catcher's mitt.
"Out!" yelled the Jets.

"She forgot to swing!" Ben cried.
"Don't you play baseball
in the circus?" Lucy yelled.
"Don't mind them," said Beezy
and Merlin.

Sarafina played right field.

Lester was up.

Lester was Home Run King
for the Jets.

Lester had a plan.

Smack! He hit the ball.

The ball sailed over Sarafina's head.

She did not move.
The ball hit the fence.
Home run for the Jets!
"I'll be ready for you
next time,"
Sarafina said.

Next time, Lester sent the ball
to right field again.

Sarafina ran.
She chased the ball
with her shark mitt.

Not fast enough!
Another home run!

"Just you wait, Lester," said Sarafina.
"You can't outsmart the shark."

Bottom of the ninth.

Lester was up again.

Bases were loaded. Two outs.

The score was tied, six to six.

Lester stepped up to the plate.

He spit on his hands.

He rubbed spit on the bat.

"Les-ter! Les-ter!" chanted the Jets.
"Wish me luck, Jaws," Sarafina said.
She had a plan. She closed her eyes.
She wished on her
alligator-tooth necklace.

Lester hit the ball.

The ball went up, up, up.

A pop fly over right field.

So high it looked like a bird.

Sarafina jumped on her unicycle.

She rode backward, eyes on the ball.

She stood up on the pedals.

She held Jaws high.

She held Jaws open.

Bam! The ball landed in her mitt.
Sarafina fell off her unicycle
with a crash.
She clamped down on the ball
with shark's teeth.
"OUT!" shouted the Hurricanes.
"Wow," said the Jets.
"Wow," said the Hurricanes.
"Who is that girl?" the Jets asked.

"Sarafina Zippy," said the Hurricanes.

"Can she play ball!"

"Let's see that shark mitt."

"Can you draw a stingray on mine?"

"After the game," Sarafina told them.

"Tenth inning. I'm up."

SELECTIONS FROM

Kick, Pass, and Run

BY Leonard Kessler

"Ready for the kickoff,"
yelled the Giants' kicker.
He kicked the football.
Up it went in the air.

A Jets' player
caught the football.
He ran up the field.

"Stop him! Tackle him!"
yelled the Giants.
"Wow," said Duck,
"that looks like fun."
She tackled Rabbit.
"Stop that," said Cat.

The Jets went into a huddle.
"The fullback
will carry the ball
around left end,"
said the quarterback.

Out of the huddle came the Jets.
"First down and ten yards to go,"
said the Jets' quarterback.
"Ready . . . Set . . . Down . . .
Hup 1 . . . Hup 2 . . . Hup 3."
The center gave him the ball.

"Hup 1 . . . Hup 2 . . . Hup 3.
Hup 1 . . . Hup 2 . . . Hup 3,"
quacked Duck.
"Oh, stop that,"
said Owl.

The quarterback
flipped the football
to the fullback.
The fullback ran five yards
before the Giants tackled him.
"Go, team, go!" quacked Duck.

Out of the huddle
came the Jets again.
"Second down
and five yards to go,"
said the quarterback.
"Ready . . . Set . . . Down . . .
Hup 1 . . . Hup 2 . . . Hup 3."
He took the ball.

• 27 •

Back. Back.

"Look out for a forward pass,"
yelled the Giants.

"Look out for a forward pass!"
yelled Frog.

Up in the air
went the football.
Down it came
to the Jets' receiver.

He caught the ball
and ran
and ran
all the way
into the end zone.

"It's a touchdown," yelled Turtle.

"Wow," said Duck.

"What's a touchdown?" asked Frog.

"A touchdown is six points," said Owl.

"Let's play football," said Cat.

SELECTIONS FROM
Practice
BY Jean Van Leeuwen
PICTURES BY Anne Schweninger

Albert could not play kickball.

He could not kick.

"Oof!" Albert missed the ball.

He could not catch.

"Uh-oh!" Albert dropped the ball.

And he could not run.

"Oops!" Albert fell over his own feet.

Oliver wished that Albert
was not on his team.

In the outfield, he stood next to him.
Each time the ball came,
Albert cried, "I've got it!"
And each time, he didn't get it.
Once the ball bounced
right on his head.

At recess every day,
Albert was sad.
"No one wants me
on their kickball team," he said.
"What you need is practice,"
said Oliver.
"Come to my house after school."

For their snack, Mother put out
a plate of peanut butter cookies.
Albert ate six.

"Wow!" said Oliver.
"Now you will have power."
"Maybe I might even kick
a home run," said Albert.

Oliver rolled the ball.

Albert kicked so hard, he fell down.

Only he missed the ball.

"Keep your eye on the ball,"
said Oliver. "That is what
my father always tells me."
"I'll try," said Albert.

"And don't look for bugs,"
said Oliver.
Oliver rolled the ball.
Albert kicked.
"I did it!" he cried.

The ball went high in the air.
Only it came right down again
and Oliver caught it.

"Phooey," said Albert. "It's an out."

"Keep trying," said Oliver.

"Remember, you have
peanut butter power."

Albert kept trying.

Sometimes he still missed.

Sometimes he kicked the ball
high in the air
and Oliver didn't catch it.
"It's a hit!" said Albert. "A real hit!"
"Good one," said Oliver.

Finally Albert kicked
a really good one.
It went over Oliver's head,
over the little pine tree,
over his sister Amanda
riding her bike in the driveway,
and into the next yard.

"Home run!" said Oliver. "Hooray!
I told you that you had
peanut butter power."
"I can't believe it," said Albert.
"A real home run!"

"Let's get a drink," said Oliver.
"Then we can practice catching."
They sat under the little pine tree
drinking lemonade.

SELECTIONS FROM

Harry's Visit

BY Barbara Ann Porte

PICTURES BY Yossi Abolafia

Jonathan is watching me.
He looks like he is making up
his mind.

"Harry," he asks, "do you want
to shoot some baskets with me
at the playground?"
Shoot some baskets?
He must be joking.
I am just a little taller
than one of Snow White's dwarfs.
"Yes," I say, "I would."

"This is Katy, Linda, Michael,
Dennis, Mary, Mollie, Max,
and Alexander,"
Jonathan tells me
when we get there.

There is a basketball court
in the playground.
It has four hoops.
Three of the hoops are very high.
One of the hoops is not so high.
"Mom made them lower it,"
says Jonathan,
"when I was your age."

Jonathan throws a ball to me.
He tells me, "Practice."
He shoots a few with me,
then joins his friends.

I play with Alexander.

"Shoot," says Alexander.

I try and miss.

"Like this," says Alexander.

I try again and miss.

"One more time,"

says Alexander.

I try very, very hard.

My ball goes through the hoop.

"Hooray," says Alexander.

"Jonathan," I shout,

"I made a basket."

"Good for you," he tells me.

"I knew that you could do it."

Fast Track

BY Nikki Grimes

PICTURE BY Henry Cole

When the whistle blows
I am ready and set
and no one can tell me
I am too anything
or less than enough.
I am a tornado of legs and feet
and warm wind whipping past
everyone else on the track
and all that's on my mind
is scissoring through
the finish line.

Soccer Sam

BY Jean Marzollo

PICTURES BY Blanche Sims

"Take Marco out to play, Sam,"
Sam's mother said.
"Introduce him to your friends."
"What if he doesn't understand
what we say?" asked Sam.
"Speak slowly," said his mom.
"He'll learn."
At the end of the street, kids were
shooting baskets. Sam's friend
Rosie tossed him the ball.
Sam aimed and fired.
The ball sailed
through the rim.

"This is my cousin Marco," Sam said.
He tried to talk slowly, but it was hard.
"Marco, this is Billy, Chris, Rosie,
Tommy, and Freddy."

Billy shot Marco the ball.
Marco caught it on his head and
bounced it up and down like a seal.
Everyone started to laugh at him.
Sam's face got hot. He grabbed
the ball and made another basket.
Chris caught the ball under the net.
He threw it to Marco.

This time Marco caught the ball on
his knee and bounced it up and down.
Again everyone laughed at him.
Sam felt awful. "Let's go home,"
he told Marco.

Back home Marco took his new
soccer ball outside.
He bounced it on his head.
He kicked it around with his feet.

Chris and Billy came over.

Marco kicked the ball to Chris.

Chris caught it with his hands.

"No hands," said Marco.

He kicked the ball to Billy.

Billy caught it with his hands too.

"No hands!" yelled Marco.

"Head! Head!" He bounced the ball
on his head.

Then Marco kicked the ball to Sam.
Sam let the ball fall on his head.
"¡Bueno!" cried Marco.
"¡Bueno, Sammee!"
Sam laughed. He kicked the ball back
to Marco, who kicked it to Billy. Billy
bounced it back to Sam with his head.

"¡Bueno Billy!" said Marco.
Then he kicked the ball to Chris.
Chris caught it on his head and
bounced it to Billy. Billy caught it
on his head and bounced it to Sam.

"This is awesome!" said Sam.
"Let's bring the ball to school
tomorrow," said Chris.
"We'll show the other kids
how to play," said Billy.
"¡Bueno!" said Marco. "Good!"

Night Game

BY Lee Bennett Hopkins

PICTURES BY Henry Cole

I'm a winner.

    A *winner.*

I never, ever lose

At any sport or game I play—

At anything I choose.

I'm a winner.

The *best* on any team.

When I'm alone
In bed at night
and dream . . .
and dream . . .
and dream.